# VAN GOGH
## THE TOUCH OF YELLOW

23

# CONTENTS

The Touch of Yellow                6

Glossary                          58

Chronology                        60

Photographic Credits              61

Cover: Self-Portrait by Van Gogh

Graphic design: Sandra Brys (Zig-Zag)

First published in the United States in 1994 by
Chelsea House Publishers.

© 1993 by Casterman, Tournai

First Printing

1  3  5  7  9  8  6  4  2

ISBN 0-7910-2817-8

ART FOR CHILDREN

# VAN GOGH

## THE TOUCH OF YELLOW

By Jacqueline Loumaye

Illustrated by Claudine Roucha

Translated by John Goodman

CHELSEA HOUSE PUBLISHERS

NEW YORK • PHILADELPHIA

# WHAT IF IT WERE A VAN GOGH?

**I** always look forward to visiting my uncle Paul. And I think he's happy to see us arrive at his mill every summer. He likes to fix up the place, and we help him out. There's plenty to do, for the building is more than 100 years old. Uncle Paul repairs the walls, climbs up on the roof, replaces the shingles, and—above all—keeps the mill wheel in perfect condition. "If need be, we could start milling grain tomorrow!" he would proudly exclaim.

This particular year, he was determined to straighten up the attic. And why not? Maybe we'd find treasure up there.

And as luck would have it, that's exactly what happened. It all started with Adam, who was coming down the stairway carrying an enormous hat box.

"Careful!" Uncle Paul cried. "You'll knock down the Van Gogh!"

Too late! The painting was on the floor, its frame broken.

"Nothing serious," said Uncle Paul. "We can easily glue it back together."

What an odd idea to hang a Van Gogh

*Still Life with Irises,*
1890.

This canvas was painted
by Van Gogh at the end
of his life. Like all his
works save one, it was
not sold during his
lifetime. A painter's
genius often goes
unrecognized until after
his or her death. Thus, a
canvas from the same
period as this one, also
of irises, was purchased
in 1987 by a private
French collector for
almost $60 million.

in a dark, upstairs hallway—especially
with Uncle Paul's love for painting. The
truth is, after a good day's work he often
takes his own easel out into the fields to
paint landscapes.

"Did you know, Uncle Paul, that a
painting of a bouquet of irises by Van
Gogh recently sold for almost sixty mil-
lion dollars?"

"Everybody knows that!" said Adam,
who knew nothing of the kind and had
never even heard of Vincent Van Gogh!

*Small Farms*, September 1883.

"Everything is beautiful here, no matter where you go."

"Why yes! He was born in a village not too far from here. Uncle Paul, you could be a millionaire if you sold your painting!"

"What do I care about that? There's no question of my selling this painting, which belonged to my grandfather the miller. It reminds me of him. And then, is it really a Van Gogh? That's still to be seen. So many tales are handed down in the family."

In any case, Uncle Paul was delighted that we were interested in his painting. No one had looked at it for a long time. We took it down into the living room where the light was better. At first all you could see was a church under a gray sky. But when we moved the painting closer to the window, the clouds above the roof began to glow.

"There seems to be a small figure in the right corner, but it's hard to make out under the thick varnish. This canvas

might have been painted in the Drente, the Northeast region of Holland. When he first started painting there, Van Gogh's palette was very dark."

"The place doesn't look too cheerful," said Adam.

"When the sun shines, it's a wild area with lots of heather. But in winter the sky clouds over and wind sweeps across the plains. That didn't prevent Van Gogh from striding through the landscape all alone. People took him for a vagrant. It was at this time that he made lots of studies of peasants at work."

"Except for the gray sky, that doesn't sound like your painting," I observed. "And there isn't even a signature."

Said Adam, "I see 'Van' in the corner."

"No! That's grass."

"I think Florence is right. In any case," Uncle Paul explained, "Van Gogh often signed with a simple 'Vincent.' But in itself that means nothing. He painted 879 paintings but signed only 130 of them. He thought it was pointless, that the only important thing was the quality of the work itself."

"He was a real original!"

It was then that Uncle Paul pulled out a magnificent book about Van Gogh. It was so heavy we had to put it on a table before we could open it. There were reproductions of all 879 paintings.

"Uncle Paul, your painting doesn't look anything like the one on the cover of the book! It can't be by the same painter," Adam said quickly.

"You're moving too fast! Painters evolve in the course of their lives," I noted.

"Like you, for example?" answered Adam, who was annoyed that I was growing much faster than he was.

"Listen to me," intervened our uncle Paul. "This particular evolution is the story of a little touch of yellow that got bigger and bigger, until it became the fireball that is the sun!"

"What little touch of yellow?"

We were both intrigued.

"That of the flames, candles, or lamps in paintings by Rembrandt and Millet, artists famous for their handling of darkness and light."

"Both at once?"

"Why yes, Horn Dog. This contrast is at the heart of the art of painting. Look closely."

Uncle Paul went to get a candle and lit it. He turned out the lamp and placed the candle on the table. In the glow of the flame, the faces of my two companions suddenly looked very different, so mysterious that one hesitated to speak. Then Uncle Paul turned on the lamp again and showed us, early on in the book, *Peasants in a Field*, painted by Van Gogh in the Drente in 1883.

"Here," Uncle Paul explained, "the little touch of yellow is only a horizontal strip of waning sunlight behind the dark profiles of peasants at work. Van Gogh was trying to capture the transitional moment of twilight in this landscape."

We looked at each other. Wasn't there a similar glow in the clouds of Uncle Paul's painting?

In any case, we had to glue the frame together. It wasn't so easy! We were just about finished when Adam said:

"I bet it's the village church!"

As if he'd never seen that our church had a high pointed steeple, while the one in the painting was quite small!

"If we can identify the church, we can

*The Angelus,* Millet, 1857.

The painter Jean-François Millet was a great influence on Van Gogh: ". . . peasant men and women are not always interesting, but when you're patient with them you see what a lot of Millet there is in these people."

determine the site and the date of this painting." Van Gogh didn't always live in Holland, Uncle Paul explained. After a few years' work there he went to Paris, and then to Arles in the south of France. In the southern sun his palette became brighter and richer.

"So it's just as you thought. The little church in our canvas was painted in Holland!" I said. "It's dark, as though night were falling."

Uncle Paul went to get his magnifying glass, and we examined the painting inch by inch. We wouldn't be arranging the attic any time soon!

"Could it be the church in Nuenen, Van Gogh's village? It's not far from here, so we can go see for ourselves! We can go by bicycle," proposed Uncle Paul.

But beforehand, he wanted to tell us about the beginning of Van Gogh's surprising story.

*Peasants in the Field,* October 1883.

"If one wants to grow one must thrust oneself into the earth. So I say to you: plant yourself in the earth of the Drente, you'll germinate there, don't wither up on the sidewalk."

Vincent Van Gogh was born on March 30, 1853 in the parsonage of Groot Zundert, the small Dutch village where his father was pastor. A year earlier to the day, his mother had given birth to another son who was stillborn, Vincent Willem. In 1853, the new child was given the same name. It was as though he had been born under the sign of death.

He had a severe upbringing, and was a taciturn child who liked to take solitary walks in marshes and fields of heather. He was interested in flowers, insects, and birds, whose nests he collected. Despite his rather wild temperament, he dreamed of having friends. But he never managed to sustain friendships with anyone for long, whether at school or later. Basically a quiet fellow, he was prone to sudden fits of anger when people disagreed with him. After he completed elementary school in the village, his father sent him to a boarding school in Zevenbergen. Vincent was once more alone. He was a mediocre student. He drew in the margins of his notebooks.

**Vincent at age 13**

He seems to have taken after his mother, who also liked to draw in her spare time. One day he gave his father a drawing for his birthday. He was only 11 years old. But as yet there was nothing to indicate he would pursue a painter's career. At age 15 his schooling came to an end. His future seemed determined. Three of his uncles were art dealers. Thanks to one of them, his uncle Cent, Vincent was hired as a salesman at Goupil, a famous picture dealer with galleries in several European cities. In July of 1869, Vincent began work in the branch in the Hague, where he was a model employee. "I earn 50 francs a month! Isn't it magnificent?"

In 1873, Theo, his younger brother, also went to work for Goupil, in Brussels. Vincent wrote to his brother: "I am so happy to know we'll both be employed in the same firm. We'll have to write to each other often now." They corresponded faithfully with one another for 17 years. Thanks to these letters we know a great deal about Van Gogh's story.

That same year, Vincent was sent to London. He visited its parks, went boating on the

**His mother**

Thames, and discovered the great English painters Constable and Turner, whose landscapes he admired. He was 20 years old, and all was well. But suddenly things took a painful turn. Ursula, the daughter of the branch manager with whom he had fallen in love, rejected him. She was already engaged. Van Gogh took this very badly. He left London and Ursula, and returned to his family. His mood was dark. Nothing interested him any more. In the spring of 1875, he was sent to the branch in Paris. He visited the galleries

and the Louvre but was now disgusted by the art market. Finally, he resigned his post and left Goupil. He returned to England, where he taught French. Vincent was looking for himself. "How can I make myself useful?" he wrote to Theo. "There's something inside me, but what is it?" Suddenly he was possessed by religious fervor. He decided to consecrate his life to God and the service of others. He would be a pastor like his father.

**His father**

**The house in Cuesmes**

Back in Holland, he decided to pursue theological studies, but they proved long and difficult. Despite all his best efforts, he failed his examinations in October 1878.

Nonetheless, that winter he was sent out to serve as a "lay evangelist" in the mining region known as the Borinage. He found himself in Wasmes, in a black country where the miners worked 12 hours a day beneath the earth. He resolved to live there like the poorest of the poor. He descended into the mines, cared for the wounded, visited the sick, and offered Bible commentary. He gave away everything he had—his money, his clothing, and his bed—sleeping on straw. These excesses displeased his superiors. In 1879 he was recalled.

But he ignored the reprimand and continued to evangelize on his own, in Cuesmes, near Mons—solitary and hungry, without authorization, money, or friends. Only Theo helped and supported him, as he would throughout his life.

*Woman Miners, 1881*

Then, Vincent confided to Theo in a letter: "I often draw late into the night to fix my memories and clarify ideas suggested to me by things I've seen." Soon Vincent would be talking of nothing but drawing in his letters.

He was 27. After years of doubt and failure, he had finally discovered his vocation. After a brief sojourn in Brussels, he returned to the region where he was born. To learn his craft, he began copying paintings by Millet. Both artists were inspired by the daily lives of workers. In August of 1881, he met a young widow, Kate Vos-Stricker, with whom he fell madly in love. Unfortunately, she was not responsive to him. In desperation, he decided to take drawing and then painting lessons with his cousin Mauve, a landscape painter. It was Mauve who gave him his first brushes and paints. From that moment forward he never stopped working.

Vincent befriended a prostitute named Sien who became his favorite model and whom he wanted to marry. Theo and the family opposed this union. Exhausted, Van Gogh fell ill. After his recovery he set to work once more, changing studios several times and reading a great deal: Zola, Hugo, Dickens. In December he returned to the family parsonage.

The next morning, we left for Nuenen. It had rained during the night but we sensed that the sun was about to come out.

"Hurry up, Florence! Uncle Paul wants to get there before noon!" cried Adam.

There was much to see. Beginning with a large linden tree over a hundred years old, surrounded by dozens of younger ones. Nearby was a large stone engraved with a sun. It bore the inscription: "Vincent Van Gogh worked in this village. December 1883–November 1885."

In order to get some idea of his work, one had only to enter a small building consecrated to him. It could have been his studio. In the center of the room was an old loom. Weavers were among Van Gogh's favorite subjects. On the wall were sketches of peasants at work. Reproductions, of course. The real ones are in museums.

"We'll go see them in Amsterdam!" promised Uncle Paul.

The summer was getting off to a great start!

Photographs of Vincent's family hung near the door: his father and mother, Willemine, Elizabeth, Anna, Cornelis.

"And Theo!" I cried. "His favorite brother!"

"Yes," said Uncle Paul. "It was thanks to Theo that Vincent was able to become an artist. Theo helped him out all his life. Vincent convinced him to try and sell his paintings in Paris. In turn, Theo encouraged him to lighten his palette to make them more saleable. But Vincent wouldn't hear of it. At that moment he saw everything in brown—the parsonage, the square tower, the cottages, and also the little church in Nuenen.

There are still 950 windmills in the low countries. Some serve, or have served, to pump water from the polders, others for the extraction of oil, the grinding of wheat, and the husking of rice and pepper.

"This reproduction isn't perfect!" Uncle Paul said of the church. "The colors are cooler than in the original."

The structure seemed less tall than in Uncle Paul's painting. Now it was time to have a look at the actual building.

After leaving, we got on our bikes and headed toward the parsonage. A priest still lived there. But we were impatient to see the church. It seemed even smaller to us than in Van Gogh's painting, as though the paints had somehow made it grander. Did it resemble the one in Uncle Paul's painting? Not really.

"Could it be a church in France, where Van Gogh went in 1886?" our uncle asked, a bit perplexed.

"I'm dying of hunger!" said Adam, who'd been carrying the picnic basket all morning.

Not far away, there was a lake. We settled down on the grass. In front of us a windmill was turning. Apparently Van Gogh painted it quite often.

The little church in Nuenen painted by Van Gogh as it appears today.

*Departing the Church in Nuenen,* January 1884.

"As regards my own color, you won't find any silvery tones in the work painted here, but rather brownish tones (for example, bitumen and sepia); I don't doubt that some will be severe with me about this."

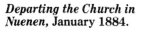

This is where we had our picnic.

nd what if we started by cleaning this painting?" Uncle Paul inquired the next day. "We'd be able to see it much better."

All we had to do, it seems, was cut a potato and rub it gently over the canvas. That made the painting much less brown. The hint of a figure disappeared, but the corner of a red roof appeared beneath a blue sky. The grass was very green and the earth blue, which was quite surprising.

"If this is Nuenen, it must be spring!" said Adam.

"The church in Nuenen doesn't have a red roof!" I pointed out.

"And what about the blue earth? Can you tell me where you'd find that?"

Uncle Paul let us bicker, but he seemed quite amused.

"And why not blue earth?" he said suddenly. "Blue like the sky. And a sky yellow like wheat! That's impressionism! Brilliant light in the sky and on the ground. In France, Renoir, Monet, and Pissarro had just reinvented painting by capturing all the nuances and reflections of light. In fact, what do you think Van Gogh did on arriving in Paris?"

"He bought new tubes of paint!" answered Adam.

"Exactly! He lightened his palette. Traditional contrasts between light and dark gave way to impressionism. Light began to vibrate in all the colors on the canvas! With certain impressionists, forms are so overwhelmed by color that it's tricky to decide what they represent! Not with Van Gogh, though, who always

*Portrait of Van Gogh,* Toulouse-Lautrec, 1887. Van Gogh served as a model for many of his painter friends. This pastel was executed by Henri de Toulouse-Lautrec at the Cormon studio, which they all frequented.

set great stock in making himself clear. He wrote: 'I am absolutely sure about my sense of color, and that it will become more and more developed. . . I have painting under my skin!' He was happy! He was living with his brother in Paris. He started to attend Cormon's studio school. He made some friends there. Henri de Toulouse-Lautrec, who thought highly of him, painted a very beautiful portrait of him. And then there was Emile Bernard, another painter who often accompanied him on his walks. But Vincent made the other students uncomfortable with his brusqueness, his thick accent, his shock of red hair, and his unkempt clothing. He worked very hard. But after three months he'd had enough. In the future he would be his own master, however difficult that might prove."

*View of Montmartre, April–June 1887.*

*View from Rue Lepic,*
**April–June 1887.**

"He was all alone again!" I said.

"Not really. For he'd moved into Theo's new apartment at 54 Lepic Street. He discovered the Montmartre hill with its kitchen gardens, windmills, and night spots, and did his best to master the light. When the weather wasn't good he worked at home, painting bouquets of flowers or the Paris rooftops visible from his window. This time, the light broke up into a thousand little points," Uncle Paul explained to us.

"Like a cloud of confetti!" said Adam.

"That's the 'pointillist' technique of

certain impressionists like Seurat and Signac, which Van Gogh used, too, but less rigorously than they did."

"It no longer looks anything like our painting," I remarked.

"Yes it does! The shutters are red, just like the roof of the church!"

"That's right! Van Gogh was sometimes audacious in his use of color for purposes of pure contrast."

Still, I wasn't convinced. That our uncle the miller could have a Van Gogh, that was just a dream! That same afternoon, without saying a word to anyone, I went exploring in the attic. I'd seen entire boxes full of old family letters up there. Might there be one signed "Vincent?" That would clarify things considerably! It started to get dark, and I had to abandon my search. When Uncle Paul saw me coming down the stairs, he was very much surprised that I'd set out to arrange the attic all alone. I didn't dare tell him that in fact I'd made things much worse!

Our project wasn't over quite yet. The inquiry continued.

"Be patient!" said Uncle Paul. "Van Gogh was still looking for himself. In Paris he painted 22 self-portraits. Including the one of him wearing a gray felt hat. Here you can see his increasing mastery of his craft. He has gone beyond the techniques of the impressionists. The point has been replaced by the short stroke. He painted this portrait with juxtaposed touches of pure color that cover the whole canvas. This is neo-impressionism, but with a pronounced personal inflection. The strokes of color form a radiant light around his face and intensify his expression.

He was right. After looking at this painting we felt we knew Van Gogh much more intimately.

"It must take a lot of time to paint with short strokes like that," said Adam.

"Not at all! Van Gogh always painted very quickly."

"Could you do a portrait of me in this style?" asked Adam.

To make him happy, Uncle Paul started his portrait. Then he let us apply the color with little brush strokes. It took us the rest of the day! Clearly we had a long way to go before mastering the technique.

"So," said Uncle Paul. "Why do you think I've drawn your attention to this style?"

We drew closer to the old painting. We hadn't yet noticed that the ground around the church was made up of just such little strokes.

"Only Van Gogh could have brought that off so well," concluded Adam.

"Careful!" said Uncle Paul. "We've

*Self-Portrait in Gray Felt Hat*, 1887.

Van Gogh painted many self-portraits; 35 are known today. They allow us to see how his painting evolved and how he used self-portraiture to increase his self-knowledge. "It is said, and I can well believe it, that it's difficult to know oneself, but it's just as difficult to paint oneself."

cleared up a few things, but can we say for sure that this painting is by Van Gogh?"

"We still don't know what church it is!" I exclaimed.

"And could that turbulent sky be over Paris?" Uncle Paul asked.

To find out, we had to wait for the rest of the story.

At the end of the 19th
century, familiarity with
Japanese art, which was
prominently displayed in
the great universal
exhibitions, encouraged
the development of new
points of view and new
ways of constructing the
image.

In Paris, Vincent and his friends regu-
larly showed their work to Père Tanguy,
a paint seller. Uncle Paul showed him to
us in his book. Van Gogh painted him in
1887.

"He looks likeable enough," said
Adam.

"Yes, indeed. In a way, all the painters
were his children. He gave them paints
because none of them could afford to buy
them. In exchange, they brought their
paintings for placement in his shop window or in a little room at the back. Works

by Signac, Seurat, Bernard, and Lautrec could all be seen there. In short, all the artists that Vincent called 'the painters of the small boulevards.' "

"And Gauguin? You haven't said a word about him."

"I'm coming to him, Adam! Van Gogh met Paul Gauguin in the fall of 1886. He had a reputation as something of an adventurer. All he could think of was trips and the tropics, which Vincent found attractive. Gauguin was a great colorist. He painted with broad strokes of bright color contained within clear outlines, as in Japanese art. This style is called 'cloisonnism' (or 'compartmentalism'). Van Gogh followed suit and began to paint in large unmodulated shapes."

"Yet another technique!" I said. "How will we ever keep track of them?"

"Also note the absence of perspective," continued Uncle Paul.

"What does that mean?" asked Adam.

"That there's no depth or relief in the painting. Everything is on the same level."

"That's no big deal! I draw like that myself!"

Adam didn't understand that doing this on purpose was a bit different.

"And why did he line up all these little pictures behind Père Tanguy?" I asked.

"Those are some of his Japanese prints. They were much admired in Paris at the time."

Adam thought that Père Tanguy, too, had something Japanese about him.

Now what was there about our own painting that made it seem "flat" in this way? We all had our ideas. But we couldn't come to an agreement.

Detail.
A Japanese print as it appears in Van Gogh's painting.

# ARLES AND THE QUEST FOR THE SUN

**T**hings were looking down for Vincent. The Parisian atmosphere no longer suited him. He fought with his friends and became angry at the slightest provocation. He drank too much.

One morning—it was February 20, 1888—he left the little apartment on Lepic Street without warning. That evening he arrived in Arles, "where there is more color, more sun." He called it "the French Japan."

"Is Arles far away, Uncle Paul?"

"It's 500 miles from Paris. When Vincent got to this town in Provence, it was covered with snow. But winter in the south of France is very different from what it is in the north. The sky above the white peaks is luminous. And spring comes very quickly. Full of enthusiasm, Vincent set to work. His impressionist palette was perfectly suited to capture the sunlight and the vivid colors of the landscape."

This made us want to follow Van Gogh to the south. Especially as it was rather cloudy that day at the mill.

"There are more Roman ruins than souvenirs of Van Gogh in Arles," Uncle Paul assured us. "I rather doubt we'd still be able to see the delicatessen he painted from the window of his room."

"This is very different from the view from the apartment on Lepic Street!"

"Absolutely! Here Van Gogh traces directly with his brush the front of the house with vertical bands of pure color. The tones are so strong that it already looks like 'fauve' or 'wild beast' painting."

"You mean like lions?" asked Adam.

*Tug-boat at Chatou,* Vlaminck, 1906.

**Van Gogh had a decisive influence on this artist, who was doubtless the "wildest" of the "wild beasts" and who, after having seen an exhibition of his predecessor's work, exclaimed: "I love Van Gogh more than my own father!"**

"What a question!"

"He's right, Florence. In one room at the Salon d'Automne or fall exhibition of 1906, some of the paintings were so violently colored that a critic called the artists 'wild beasts.' The painters in question included Maurice Vlaminck and Henri Matisse. Van Gogh used pure color right out of the tube much earlier than they did."

"So how can we see how our little touch of yellow got bigger under the sun of Provence?"

"Simple!" said Uncle Paul. "We'll go to the museum in Amsterdam."

At our insistence, he arranged a meeting to show our painting to a curator there. We were supposed to bring a photograph of the work to make his job easier.

"Why don't you just take the painting with you, Uncle Paul?" asked Adam.

"What if I left it in the checkroom with the umbrellas?"

*The Delicatessen,*
February 1888.

"It sometimes seems to me that my blood is more or less trying to circulate again, which it hasn't been doing recently in Paris, I'm really sick of the place."

# "HIS" MUSEUM

We arrived at the famous Vincent Van Gogh Museum. The whole world passes through its doors! And in poor Vincent's lifetime nobody appreciated his painting. What sweet revenge!

After we entered, to the right there was a room full of documents and information about Van Gogh.

A young woman greeted us.

"The curator would like a little time to research your painting. Could you come back in two days?"

We were a bit disappointed about the delay, but Adam wasn't going to waste any time.

"And what do you think?" he asked.

"I hope, for your sake, that it's a Van Gogh," she said hesitantly, with a hint of irony.

Why this ironic smile, and why had Uncle Paul said we mustn't impose too much on the curator? It isn't every day that a new Van Gogh is discovered!

*The Potato Eaters,*
**April–May 1885.**

"For my part, I'm convinced that in the long run one gets better results painting them in all their crudity rather than softening them to agree with convention. . . . If a painting of peasants smells of lard, smoke, and potatoes, that's perfect!"

We kept our spirits up. While awaiting the verdict, we went to look at the Van Goghs in the museum, beginning at the beginning. The paintings of the Drente and Nuenen, with the masterpiece of the Dutch period,—The Potato Eaters—. They're all seated around a table, eating from a single plate.

Uncle Paul said these peasants' faces reminded him of dirty potatoes! That was going too far! But Van Gogh was so successful in conveying, under the dim glow of the lamp, the harsh reality of these lives that this work already seems "expressionist." The expressionist movement in painting came much later. Van Gogh was one of the first people to use its techniques. First, because of the emphatic structure of his paintings. The lines are solid and the surfaces well defined. But above all, beginning in this painting, because of the force with which he "expressed" his intention, showing us real peasants in all their solidity and crudeness. Somehow we sense that he appreciated them for these qualities.

"It's as though they're about to jump off the canvas!" said Adam, lurching backward.

And yet, one of the peasants looked at the others with such gentleness that you forgot they had only potatoes to eat. Suddenly the meal seemed quite sumptuous!

*Study.*
A dozen preparatory studies for *The Potato Eaters* exist, and there are three versions of the painting: two with five peasants and one with only four.

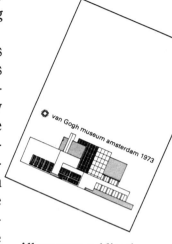

All museum publications carry this trademark representing the building.

"Remember that in 1888, after a harsh winter in Arles, Van Gogh finally saw the southern spring in all its gaiety. A blustery wind swept the clouds through the sky. All the orchards were in bloom! Overcome with wonder, he planted his easel in the countryside—solidly, so the wind couldn't blow it away. He painted 10 orchard pictures in a flash! Every day he got to know Arles and its red roof tiles a little better. Here you can even see the city hall through the trees."

"What's that bell-tower beyond the orchard?" asked Adam. "Doesn't it look like the one in our painting?"

"That's the tower of the church of Saint-Trophime, famous for its cloister, the oldest in Provence. I think the one in our painting belongs to a small village church."

"You must have been to Arles!" I said to Uncle Paul.

"Yes, a long time ago. Unfortunately, the orchards were not in bloom. But isn't the brilliance of the light so well captured here that you can imagine you're in the middle of Provence?"

"It smells good," said Adam, his nose close to the canvas. "Like cherries!"

His investigations had led him to conclude they were cherry trees. Could it be he was right?

The church of Saint-Trophime

While Uncle Paul was still pondering whether they might not be pear trees, we discovered another painting we liked.

"That's funny," said Adam, "it looks like Holland!"

"Except for the colors," I added, thinking of the landscape we'd seen from the train.

"There's a lot of yellow!" said Uncle Paul, joining us. "It's summer. The hay has been cut. The little touch of yellow has gotten much bigger! It's even in the blue sky, making for that amazing green color! 'Some old gold, some bronze, some copper under the azure green of a sky keyed up with white,' in Van Gogh's own words. Look at the large blocks of color, clearly shown as in the Japanese landscapes that Van Gogh so loved. On the other hand, the foreground is brushed in with small separate strokes with a technique inherited from the impressionists."

While Adam was counting the wagons,

[in handwritten script]
I wrote to the Tourism Office in Arles. The city doesn't have any paintings by Van Gogh, but the folders they sent me suggest the city is very beautiful.

J'ai écrit à l'Office du Tourisme d'Arles. La ville ne possède pas de tableaux de Van Gogh mais, d'après les documents envoyés, la cité a l'air bien belle.

ladders, and horses, I moved up closer to the canvas. I was as dazzled by the sun as Van Gogh had been, and so absorbed that I hadn't noticed a small group of visitors around us. They mistook Uncle Paul for a museum guide!

*Harvest—The Plain of La Crau*, June 1888.

"Our own Van Gogh isn't quite so luminous," he concluded.

"You own a Van Gogh?" asked a man with a low voice. "Make sure a thief doesn't make off with it!"

We hadn't thought of that! Uncle Paul couldn't remember whether he'd locked the kitchen door.

***The Yellow House,*** **1888.
On arriving in Arles, Van
Gogh settled in a hotel
close to the train
station. A few months
later he rented this
house on the Place
Lamartine. It was here
that he hoped to house a
group of artist friends.
The neighborhood was
seriously damaged by
bombs during World War
II, and this house was
unfortunately destroyed.**

View of Arles at the end of the 19th century.

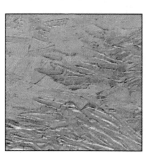

"And here's the yellow house," announced Uncle Paul. "A house the color of the sun! Van Gogh came to love yellow more and more. 'A sun,' he wrote Theo, 'a light that, for want of a better word, I will call yellow, pale saffron yellow, pale lemon, gold. How beautiful yellow is!'"

"The sky is the same blue as in your painting!" I remarked.

Uncle Paul moved in for a close look, his glasses on the tip of his nose.

"The sky here is smoother, but in fact it's the same saturated blue. Look at the brutal color contrast Vincent used to express himself with greater force."

"That's different from impressionism?" I asked.

"Absolutely! Within a few months, Van Gogh had unlearned everything he'd picked up in Paris."

"So what good did it do him?" inquired Adam.

"It was a new experiment for him. But you'll soon see that Van Gogh's painting continued to evolve."

***The Artist's Bedroom at
Arles,*** **October 1888.**
**"The walls are pale
violet. The flooring is
red. The wood of the bed
and chairs is fresh butter
yellow, the sheets and
pillows a very light
greenish citron. The
bedspread bright red.
The window green. The
toilette table orangish,
the washbasin blue. The
doors lilac. And that's it,
there's nothing else in
this bedroom with its
shutters closed. The
broad lines of the
furniture again must
express inviolable
repose."**

We moved on a few steps, and it was
as though we had entered Vincent's
house! His bedroom was yellow—sunlit
and quite simple, with just a bed, a table,
and two chairs. But Theo had to pay for
the furniture. Vincent was so poor that
he wasn't sure he could afford to buy a
bed. He considered renting one because
it was much cheaper! But he also had to
arrange the rest of the house for the
arrival of his friend Gauguin. Van Gogh so
admired Gauguin that he invited Paul to
live with him in Arles. While waiting for
Gauguin, Van Gogh went into the fields
to gather the big flowers called "sunflowers" because they always turn toward the

*Les tournesols
sont fort appré-
ciés dans notre
pays et pourtant
c'est en Provence
que Van Gogh
commença à
les peindre.*

sun. He made bouquets and painted them to decorate his friend's bedroom.

"He dreamed of founding a studio of the south where all painters in love with the sun could work together!" Uncle Paul told us.

"What a great idea!"

"Yes!" he answered me. "But unfortunately things didn't work out. Van Gogh and Gauguin began to argue, falling into violent disagreements about the subject matter of their paintings. Van Gogh didn't like to be contradicted, and he was wounded by his guest's statements that Vincent owed everything to him, including the range of brilliant yellows in his sunflower pictures."

Adam was so enthusiastic that he wanted to paint his bedroom yellow when we got back!

**Sunflowers, 1888.**

**"I'm painting with the heartiness of a Marseillais eating fish stew, which won't surprise you because I'm painting large sunflowers."**

*En sortant du musée, nous avons été au marché aux fleurs.*

*Pour s'amuser, Oncle Paul en a acheté un bouquet avec un billet de 50 gulden, orné de tournesols.*

"And do you know what happened?" asked Uncle Paul. "On the evening of December 23, 1888, when all Arles was getting ready to celebrate Christmas, Gauguin went out alone after dinner. It was cold and there was a biting wind. Suddenly he heard jerky steps behind him. Vincent was coming at him with a razor! But he stopped himself and returned to the yellow house. Understandably frightened, Gauguin spent the night in a hotel. The next day a crowd gathered in front of the house. The police interrogated Gauguin, for there was blood everywhere! Vincent had cut off his ear with the razor! And that's not all! He had wrapped it up and taken it to a friend of his named Rachel!"

"That's a very strange gift!" I said, slightly disgusted.

Uncle Paul added that he then went to the Arles hospital to consult a Dr. Rey.

"All that because he had a fight with his best friend!" sighed Adam.

"It was said that he wanted to punish himself for assaulting Gauguin. Theo was devastated. Were these the early signs of serious illness? The inhabitants of Arles, who took him for a dangerous madman, wanted the bandaged stranger locked up. The studio of the south was finished. A

*Self-portrait with Bandaged Ear and Pipe,* January 1889.

"Let me calmly continue my work, if it's that of a madman, then so be it. I can't do anything about that."

month later, all alone, he completed a self-portrait with his ear bandaged. He would use painting to fend off his madness."

This portrait wasn't in the museum. But we saw a postcard of it in the bookstore downstairs. Adam bought a copy to decorate his future yellow bedroom.

Meanwhile, I was picking out a few postcards for myself. We had to line up, for there were lots of kids doing the same thing. If they'd been asked for their opinion a hundred years ago, Van Gogh would have become famous right away!

*The Rhone River at Night,* September 1888.

"That doesn't prevent me from having a terrible need for, dare I say the word, religion, so I go out at night to paint the stars and I always dream of a painting like this with the lively figures of a couple."

That evening we took a walk through Amsterdam under a starry sky. We crossed a dozen little bridges. The light from the street lamps illuminated the facades, which were reflected in the water. We heard the bells of bicycles winding through the crowd. Tour boats glided down the canals. There were musicians, singers, and mimes on the corners and in the squares.

*Starry Night,* June 1889.

Almost a year later Van Gogh painted a new version of a starry night, more agitated and tormented.

We could have kept walking all night, it was so festive.

"Van Gogh also loved the starry night sky!" said Uncle Paul. "Don't you remember? In the book there was a reproduction of a night over Arles. But that particular painting is in Paris."

"How can one paint the night when one so loves the sun?" asked Adam.

"Because if you look closely you'll see that the night is full of colors. Blue, green, and violet emerge beneath the twinkling of the stars, and even in the lights of the city."

Myself, I thought the Amsterdam sky must be very different from that in Arles, for even when I strained my eyes I couldn't see any green!

"But yes! In the halos around each star!" asserted Uncle Paul, whose painter's eye was doubtless sharper than ours.

"You have magic eyes!" proclaimed Adam.

"In any case, I understand Van Gogh. I love to walk under the stars. It's at such moments that I feel the immensity of the universe, and our own puniness."

Then Uncle Paul added, all excited: "I've just remembered a painting of a starry night. It's in the museum in Otterloo. It's decided! Tomorrow we'll go there. I saw that our hotel sponsors trips to the park in which it's situated. I don't think you'll regret it! Then we'll go back to the Amsterdam museum."

Uncle Paul is a really great guy!

En nous promenant à Amsterdam, nous avons découvert une petite bouteille d'advokaat portant le nom de Van Gogh dans une boutique encore ouverte.

[in handwritten script]
While exploring Amsterdam we discovered a little bottle of Advokaat bearing the name of Van Gogh in a boutique.

# AN INDISPENSABLE EXCURSION

A car brought us to the gates of the park, and we rented bicycles for the rest of the trip. We passed through pine forests and mist-covered heaths like those beloved of Van Gogh. The road edged around lakes full of all kinds of birds.

"With a little luck we might also see some deer," Uncle Paul announced. "This park is a nature preserve."

But we could already make out the museum amidst the trees, as well as a big red K on the lawn.

"For Kröller-Müller, the name of the museum's founder," Uncle Paul explained.

Inside, everything was white and light penetrated through large windows looking onto the garden. There were Van Goghs in the very first rooms.

"Ah! —The Sower—!" said Uncle Paul. "This painting was done in Arles, but the gesture of such workers is the same in Holland and in Provence. Van Gogh never got tired of painting it."

"The birds are following him to eat the

seed!" said Adam, who always noticed the details.

"Those are crows. There's something threatening about their little black marks in the sunlight. And yet at this moment he was painting contentedly."

"Have we looked to see if there's a raven hidden somewhere in our painting?" asked Adam.

No one could remember seeing one. At that moment we noticed an empty spot on the wall.

"Just the place to hang our painting!" declared Adam.

"But we're still not sure it was painted in Arles," I said.

"We don't even know if Van Gogh painted it at all!" Uncle Paul added, as though suddenly concerned that the painting might be leaving his mill.

Sculpture at the entrance in the form of a K.

The Sower, August 1888.

"For a long time now I've wanted to do a sower, but my long-standing desires don't always get realized. So I'm a little afraid. And yet after Millet and Lhermitte, what has yet to be done is . . . a *Sower* with color and in a large format." In his letters, Vincent often drew sketches of his future paintings (see detail, above).

When we arrived in front of *Sidewalk Cafe at Night,* at first Adam and I were surprised. It was so different from *The Rhone River at Night,* reproduced in Uncle Paul's book! Here the sky was quite small and had far fewer stars.

"This was the first time he painted at night. So he started with a little patch of sky and took advantage of the lights of the cafe. It's even said that sometimes he lit candles on his hat! So some called him 'lit up' or 'illuminé' in French, which also means crazy."

"They were idiots," I said.

At that moment we heard laughter behind us. It was two little girls with their grandmother.

"Now don't get distracted! Listen to me instead!" she told them. "Look at the stars in this painting. They're little candles in the sky!"

Their grandmother was right. Van Gogh surely didn't need any candles on his hat!

"That's not a grandmother, that's at *least* a *great* grandmother!" Adam whispered to me.

But so what? If she lived at the same time as Van Gogh, she probably knows what she's talking about!

"The most important thing in this painting," interrupted Uncle Paul, "is the brilliant patch of yellow contrasting with the deep blue of the city and sky. And the twinkling fire of the stars."

Their effectiveness had us all in agreement for once!

*Sidewalk Cafe at Night,*
September 1888.
"To express hope by
means of some star."
[sic. Editor]

*Road with Cypress and Star,* May 1890.

"Cypresses still preoccupy me. . . . They're beautiful like Egyptian obelisks. And their green has a certain distinguished quality. They're black stains in a sunny landscape, but they're among the most interesting black notes, the most difficult to get right, that I can imagine."

Adam ran ahead of us. Imperturbable, Uncle Paul continued to play the tour guide, and each time we stopped, more and more peopled joined us. Uncle Paul should try for a job at a museum!

"The butt of hostility, Van Gogh suffered from loneliness and stumbled from crisis to crisis. In May of 1889, he asked Theo to have him admitted to the asylum of Saint-Rémy in Provence on condition that he be permitted to paint, even behind the bars of his window. He was even allowed to paint in the immediate vicinity of the asylum, accompanied by a guardian.

"In Saint-Rémy his style became more and more agitated, and his touch disturbingly sinuous. Some have seen this style as proof of his madness. But Vincent said it was just the result of his observation of nature. One day he was allowed to go for a walk along a road lined with cypresses, a typical sight in the southern landscape. The weather was stormy. The sun had almost completely disappeared behind the clouds. The great flame of one of these trees was given the central place in the painting."

I was beginning to understand that Uncle Paul was right to be concerned. The little black spots of the crows over the wheat fields had gotten much bigger.

"Vincent wasn't really happy," he told us. "In close quarters with inmates who often screamed or trembled, he tried to escape from his anxieties through work.

"But he lacked freedom, models, and space. He confided to Theo his wish to leave the Saint-Rémy asylum. In Auvers-sur-Oise, near Paris, there lived a Dr. Gachet who was a great friend of the impressionists. Perhaps he could help his brother."

While Uncle Paul was speaking, I saw that Adam was really hypnotized by the cypress tree. I had to shake him to get him to move. He gave me a very strange look, as if he were coming out of a nightmare.

Then Uncle Paul decided it was time to go outside. After leaving the museum, we bicycled for some time amidst the dunes and the trees, hoping to see some deer. And suddenly there they were, 30 feet in front of us! A small herd calmly crossing a clearing.

At that moment the tormented nature of Van Gogh seemed very remote!

The house of Doctor Gachet.

***Portrait of Doctor Gachet,*** June 1890.

"To me he seems as sick as you or I, and he's older . . . but he's very much the doctor, and his profession and his faith keep him going."

# IN AUVERS,
## MAD WITH PAINTING

hile taking us back to the Amsterdam museum, Uncle Paul confirmed that Vincent soon went to Auvers, where the sun was less intense, less brilliant than in the south. He needed quiet and repose. He arrived in Paris for a brief stay on the morning of May 17, 1890. There he met Theo's wife, Johanna, for the first time as well as their baby, the little Vincent whose godfather he was. In a hurry to begin painting once more, he left for Auvers three days later. He settled over the cafe in the town square, which was run by the Ravoux family, and set to work immediately.

The cafe on the town square in Auvers-sur-Oise, where Van Gogh lived.

In our own impatience we had arrived an hour too early. Uncle Paul wanted to show us a painting that was all yellow, painted in Saint-Rémy during the harvest.

Adam found the little reaper immediately.

"Is he going to do all the work himself? Impossible!" he said.

"This courageous little man attacking an immense wheat field is meant to be Vincent himself. The sun inflames both sky and earth like a kind of wildfire!"

"Our little touch of yellow has become a ball of fire, the sun!" I was recalling what Uncle Paul had told us some days ago.

He couldn't help admiring the beautiful color of the ripe wheat. It must have made him think of his mill, and a time when grain was milled there.

"Van Gogh was ravished by Auvers," he told us. "His colors glow from the canvas, but without violence, for the landscape of the region surrounding Paris is less arid than that of Provence, and its light is less relentless. Vincent felt well and each day discovered a new corner of this pretty village on the banks of the Oise. His life suddenly seemed full of happiness and contentment amidst the kind of simple people he loved. He also saw Dr. Gachet quite often, who invited him to dine. They talked together about painting."

"Like us!" said Adam, with a self-important air.

*The Reaper*, September 1889.

"There! *The Reaper* is finished. . . . It's an image of death as the great book of nature speaks of it, but what I've tried for is the 'almost smiling.' It's all yellow, except for a line of violet hills, a pale, fair yellow."

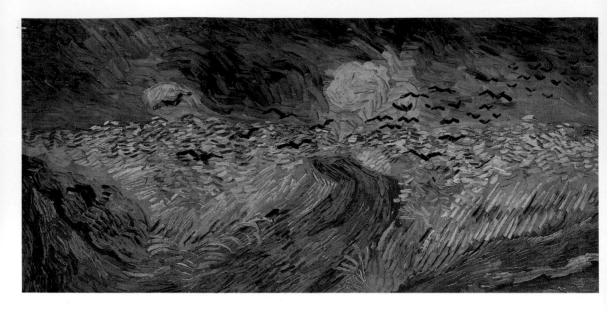

*Crows over the Wheat Field,* July 1890.

"The fact is we can only speak through our paintings." (Last letter from Vincent to Theo).

"Van Gogh was free once more! And he was discovering the beautiful landscape of Auvers."

"The sky is deep blue like in Provence," remarked Adam.

"No, those are storm clouds. From about early July, they also began to accumulate in Vincent's life. He was once again becoming anxious."

"Despite Dr. Gachet and the friends looking after him?" I asked.

"The doctor was a disappointment, even though he invited him to dinner. It seems their discussions had taken on an unpleasant edge, as both were irritable men. And Vincent had discovered that his brother Theo was having such a hard time at work that he was thinking of leaving Goupil. If he did, how would he be able to help out Vincent? To make matters even worse, his godson had fallen sick. Everything suddenly seemed black. His touch became agitated again, and the wheat fields he loved now resembled the waves of a rough sea about to sweep him away."

While looking at this painting, the sky began to seem very heavy and dark. And the fields deserted. The wind blew all around us and the black crows brushed us with their wings as they cried out.

"They're enormous!" Adam whispered in my ear.

Even the thick yellow strokes of the wheat seemed sinister.

"Careful! Don't get lost!"

It was the voice of Uncle Paul.

"Come back!"

Why was he yelling like that in the museum?

"Me? I'm not yelling!" he said with surprise. "I was just pointing out that this roadway leads nowhere."

"Did you notice, Uncle Paul? This road turns just like the one in your painting!" I said.

"No!" he answered firmly. "This one gets lost in the wheat."

He opened the catalogue he was carrying to its last page:

July 27, 1890. Night has fallen. Vincent staggers up to his room. He spreads out on his iron bed in his clothes. He's in great pain. There's a bloodstain on his shirt. While alone in the fields he had shot himself in the chest. But he managed to make it back to his room in the inn, and Dr. Gachet was called. He hesitated to act, for the bullet would be difficult to remove. Vincent became weaker but was suffering less. He lit a pipe and waited for Theo, who had been informed. They spent his last hours together. "Dying is difficult, but living is still more difficult," Vincent had said by his father's deathbed. Theo now remembered these words. He didn't say much in order not to fatigue his brother. "You'll recover," he said, "and you won't have any more attacks." "It's useless, the sadness will always remain," Vincent answered. All was calm. A few moments later he closed his eyes for the last time. He was thirty-seven.

Uncle Paul grew quiet. We moved away from the painting. The black crows were flying away and would soon disappear into the setting sun. "With my work, I risk my life, and I've sacrificed half my reason to it," Van Gogh wrote in the last letter addressed to his brother.

It was time to return to the curator's office. We descended the stairs without saying a word. He was waiting for us.

"Sit down!" he said gently. "I've had a look at the photo of your painting."

He went to get a large book entitled *Van Gogh in Auvers-sur-Oise* and showed us the church in Auvers as painted by Van Gogh.

"Oh! The red roof!" cried Adam.

"And the two paths!" I added. "But there isn't a figure in our painting."

"Quite true." said Uncle Paul, as if he'd known it for some time.

"So?" asked Adam.

"So?" repeated Uncle Paul.

"Well," said the curator, "it's certainly not a Van Gogh, but many painters worked in Auvers-sur-Oise, attracted by this charming village on the riverbank— Daubigny, Pissarro, Cézanne, Renoir, and many others who are less well known. It could well be that one of them did your painting, for the handling is cer- tainly impressionist. I wouldn't be the

*The Church at Auvers-sur-Oise,* June 1890.

least bit surprised. But you must ask an expert about that."

"I suppose that's what we should have done at the beginning," said Uncle Paul. "I never really believed it could be a Van Gogh, but the children were so insistent and you were so kind about seeing us despite the doubts I expressed to you."

"There's no need to apologize. The work is interesting even if it's by an unknown painter. It's worth looking into."

"So our search isn't over yet!" Adam concluded happily.

As for myself, I was rather disappointed that it wasn't a Van Gogh. But in the end that's not so important, for thanks to this canvas we got to know a remarkable painter.

Theo died not long after Vincent. A few years later his remains were moved to a spot beside his brother's, in Auvers.

# GLOSSARY

**Cézanne, Paul (1839–1906):** French painter whose daring use of color and form influenced many modern abstract painters.

**Gauguin, Paul (1848–1903):** French painter known for his use of bright, unshaded colors and the tropical settings of many of his later paintings.

**Montmartre:** neighborhood in the hilly, northern part of Paris known for its nightclubs and cabarets, the beautiful Church of the Sacred Heart, and the city's largest collection of street painters.

**Oise River:** a river in northern France that flows southwest toward Paris and the Seine River.

**Pissarro Camille (1830–1903):** French impressionist painter known primarily for his depictions of peasant life and the French countryside.

Along the walkway, passersby can admire the beautiful flowers that fill the open air boutiques and the numerous sailboats along the pier that have been transformed into floating greenhouses.

The Lediestraat is a great pedestrian walkway in Amsterdam. One of its main attractions are the shops full of the beautiful wooden shoes so typical of the country.

**Provence:** region of southeastern France bordering on the Mediterranean sea.

**Rembrandt Harmensz van Rijn (1606–1669):** Dutch painter whose dark, shadowy portraits are among the greatest ever produced.

**Renoir, Pierre-Auguste (1841–1919):** the greatest portrait painter of late–19th-century France.

**Seurat, Georges (1858–1891):** Parisian impressionist painter who used colorful dots to depict the beautiful parks and landscapes around Paris.

**Toulouse-Lautrec, Henri-Marie Raymond de (1864–1901):** impressionist painter and poster designer known for his dramatic scenes of Parisian nightlife.

Saint-Rémy-de-Provence is another interesting place to visit, notable for its rustic cloisters.

In the garden behind the Kröller-Müller Museum, there are modern scupltures by artists like Claus Oldenburg and Jean Dubuffet.

# Chronology

| | |
|---|---|
| 1853 | Vincent Van Gogh is born in Groot Zundert in the Dutch Brabant |
| 1869 | Hired by the Goupil Gallery in the Hague |
| 1873 | Works at the Goupil branch in London |
| 1874 | Transfers to the Goupil branch in Paris |
| 1879 | Becomes a lay evangelist in the Borinage |
| 1880 | Studies drawing in Antwerp |
| 1881 | Moves to the Hague and works with the painter Mauve, his cousin |
| 1883 | Leaves his companion Sien; rejoins his family in Nuenen |
| 1885 | Paints *The Potato Eaters* |
| 1886 | Settles in Paris; studies at Cormon's studio school; meets Toulouse-Lautrec, Pissarro, Signac, and Gauguin |
| 1888 | Sojourns in Arles; paints *The Artist's Bedroom, The Yellow House,* and a wheat field series; first attack of madness |
| 1889 | From May 8, lives in the hospital of Saint-Rémy-de-Provence; paints *Irises, Cypresses* |
| 1890 | From the end of May, stays in Auvers-sur-Oise with Doctor Gachet; paints *Portrait of Doctor Gachet, Crows Over the Wheat Field*; commits suicide on July 27 |

# Where Are the Paintings by Van Gogh?

IN THE VAN GOGH FOUNDATION, VINCENT VAN GOGH NATIONAL MUSEUM, AMSTERDAM:
p. 7 *Still Life with Irises.*
p. 8 *Small Farms.*
p. 11 *Peasants in the Field.*
p. 17 *Departing the Church in Nuenen.*
p. 19 *View of Montmartre.*
p. 29 *View from Rue Lepic.*
p. 30 *The Potato Eaters.*
p. 32 *Orchard in Bloom with View of Arles.*
p. 35 *Harvest—The Plain of La Crau.*
p. 36 *The Yellow House.*
p. 38 *The Artist's Bedroom at Arles.*
p. 39 *Sunflowers.*
p. 53 *The Reaper.*
p. 54 *Crows over the Wheat Field.*
Cover *Self-Portrait.*

IN THE KRÖLLER-MÜLLER FOUNDATION, OTTERLOO:
p. 15 *Woman Miners.*
p. 45 *The Sower.*
p. 47 *Sidewalk Cafe at Night.*
p. 48 *Road with Cypress and Star.*

IN THE ORSAY MUSEUM, PARIS:
p. 42 *The Rhone River at Night.*
p. 51 *Portrait of Doctor Gachet.*
p. 57 *The Church at Auvers-sur-Oise.*

IN THE MUSÉE RODIN, PARIS:
p. 24 *Portrait of Père Tanguy.*

IN THE KUNSTHAUS, MUNICH:
p. 29 *The Postman Roulin.*

IN THE MUSEUM OF MODERN ART, NEW YORK:
p. 42: *Starry Night.*

IN THE LEIGH-BLOCK COLLECTION, CHICAGO:
p. 41 *Self-Portrait with Bandaged Ear and Pipe.*

*The Angelus* by Millet is in the Orsay Museum, Paris.
*Tugboat at Chatou* by Vlaminck is in a private collection in Basle, Switzerland.
The *Portrait of Van Gogh* by Toulouse-Lautrec is in the Stedelijk Museum in Amsterdam.

# Photographic Credits

Van Gogh Foundation, Vincent Van Gogh National Museum, Amsterdam: pp. 8, 11, 12, 13, 17, 18, 19, 20, 23, 27, 30, 31, 32, 35, 36, 38, 39, 47, 53, 54.
Stichting Kröller-Müller, Otterloo: pp. 15, 44, 45, 48.
Reunion des Musées Nationaux, Paris: pp. 24, 25.
Museum of Modern Art, New York: p. 42 (bottom).
Roger-Viollet: pp. 7, 37, 41, 52.
Giraudon: pp. 26, 29.

Quotations from Van Gogh's letters in the captions are translated from *Lettres de Vincent Van Gogh à son frere Théo*, Grasset, 1937.